Arlin

Treats For Young Readers Series, Volume 2

Dylan Simphiwe Ncube

Published by Leanshake DPT. Of Literal Arts, 2024.

This is a work of fiction. Similarities to real people, places, or events are entirely coincidental.

ARLIN

First edition. December 21, 2024.

ISBN: 979-8230901228

Written by Dylan Simphiwe Ncube.

Also by Dylan Simphiwe Ncube

Treats For Young Readers Series
The Magic Paintbrush
Arlin

Watch for more at https://leansavagemerch.teemill.com/.

Table of Contents

Myself

Don't just memorize the words, comprehend the meaning

Chapter 1

Arlin hunched over his desk, surrounded by stacks of dusty tomes and scattered notes, like a scholar possessed by the ghosts of ancient wisdom. His small, cluttered bedroom was a testament to his love for learning, with shelves overflowing like a bibliophile's treasure trove. The air was thick with the musty scent of old books and the faint hint of ozone, as if the very atmosphere was charged with magical energy.

As a novice wizard, Arlin spent most of his free time studying magic theory and practicing spells, fueled by a determination that bordered on obsession. His eyes, a deep, rich brown, shone with an intensity that belied his youth, like two stars burning brightly in the darkness.

His mother, Elara, knocked softly on the door, her voice a gentle melody that pierced the silence. "Arlin, dinner's ready. Come down, dear."

Arlin sighed, marking his place in the current book with a dog-eared corner. "Coming, Mom," he muttered, his tone a perfect blend of teenage apathy and reluctant obedience.

As he entered the kitchen, the aroma of roasted chicken and steaming vegetables enveloped him, a savory symphony that tantalized his taste buds. Elara smiled weakly, her dark skin sallow from her ongoing illness, like a moon eclipsed by a shadow.

"Arlin, I'm worried about you," Elara said, concern etched on her face like a fine pen and ink drawing. "You're spending too much time cooped up in your room. You need to get out more, feel the sun on your face, and the wind in your hair."

Arlin shifted uncomfortably, his eyes darting around the kitchen like a trapped animal seeking escape. "I'm fine, Mom. I just need to focus on my studies. I promise I'll take breaks and get some fresh air... eventually."

Elara's gaze lingered on her son, her eyes searching for any sign of reassurance. "Okay, dear. But promise me you'll be careful. Magic can be unpredictable, and I don't want you to get hurt."

Arlin nodded, feeling a pang of guilt, like a remorseful Judas. He knew his mother worried about him, but he couldn't help his drive to master magic. The Orb of Light, with its rumored healing properties, seemed like the only hope to save his mother from the ravages of her illness.

As they ate dinner, Arlin's thoughts drifted back to his research, his mind consumed by the thrill of the hunt. He devoured books on magic theory, pouring over ancient texts like a starving man at a feast. The words danced on the page, a cryptic language that only he could decipher.

Little did Arlin know, his life was about to take a dramatic turn, like a ship sailing into a stormy night. The winds of fate were gathering, and he was about to embark on a journey that would test his courage, his wits, and his very soul.

Arlin stepped out of his front door, taking a deep breath of the crisp morning air. The sun was rising over the rooftops, casting a warm glow over the quiet neighborhood. He shouldered his backpack, loaded with books and notes, and set off towards the city center.

As he walked, he stumbled upon a street performer juggling clubs while riding a unicycle. Arlin watched, mesmerized, as the performer expertly juggled the clubs while maintaining a witty banter with the crowd.

Arlin tossed a few coins into the performer's tip jar and continued on his way. He arrived at the small, unassuming shop tucked away on a side street. The sign above the door read "Curios and Antiques," but Arlin knew it was more than that. This was the place where he met his mentor, Ryan.

Arlin pushed open the door, and a bell above it rang out, announcing his arrival. The shop was dimly lit, the air thick with the scent of old books and dust. Ryan looked up from behind the counter, his eyes twinkling with warmth.

"Ah, Arlin! Right on time. I've got a new text for you to study." Ryan handed Arlin a slim, leather-bound book. "This one's on advanced spellcasting. I think you're ready for it."

Arlin took the book, his fingers tracing the intricate symbols etched into the cover. "Thanks, Ryan. I'll study it carefully."

Ryan nodded, his expression serious. "Remember, Arlin, magic's not just about casting spells. It's about understanding the underlying principles, the balance of energies. Don't just memorize the words; comprehend the meaning."

Arlin nodded, feeling a sense of determination. He was ready to learn, to master the arcane arts. The Orb of Light was within his grasp, and he wouldn't let anything stand in his way.

As they chatted, a customer entered the shop, browsing the shelves. Ryan excused himself to assist the customer, leaving Arlin to browse the shelves.

Arlin's eyes landed on a peculiar-looking artifact – a small, crystal orb with an intricate network of silver filigree. He picked it up, feeling an unexpected surge of energy.

Ryan returned, noticing Arlin's fascination with the orb. "Ah, you've found the Starlight Orb. That's a rare and powerful artifact."

Arlin's eyes widened. "What does it do?"

Ryan chuckled. "Well, that's a story for another time. Let's just say it's not for beginners."

Arlin carefully returned the orb to its shelf, his mind racing with possibilities.

As he prepared to leave, Ryan called out, "Arlin, don't forget to practice your spells. And don't blow anything up, okay?"

Arlin grinned, shouldering his backpack. "I'll try my best."

With a wave, Arlin stepped out into the bright sunlight, ready to face whatever magical adventures lay ahead.

Chapter 2

Arlin settled into his favorite armchair, surrounded by stacks of dusty tomes and scattered notes. The soft glow of the lamp cast a warm light on the pages of the book Ryan had given him. He delved into the world of advanced spellcasting, devouring the words like a starving man at a feast.

As he read, Arlin's mind wandered to the Orb of Light. What secrets lay hidden within its ancient, mystical energies? He felt an inexplicable connection to the artifact, as if it held the key to unlocking the mysteries of the universe.

Arlin's research led him to an obscure text, penned by a mysterious sorceress named Aria. The words danced on the page, speaking of the Orb's power to heal even the most grievous of wounds.

"...the Orb of Light, forged in the heart of the ancient world, holds the essence of creation. Its power, boundless and pure, can mend the fabric of reality itself."

Arlin's eyes widened as he read the passage. Could it be true? Could the Orb of Light really heal his mother's affliction?

With newfound determination, Arlin continued his research, pouring over ancient texts and scouring the internet for any mention of the Orb. The hours ticked by, the sun dipping below the horizon as Arlin's obsession grew.

As the night wore on, Arlin's phone buzzed, breaking the silence. He glanced at the screen, a text from Ryan flashing on the display.

"Meet me at the shop tomorrow. I have something to show you."

Arlin's heart skipped a beat. What could Ryan have in store for him? He couldn't wait to find out.

Arlin walked into the shop, the bell above the door jingling merrily. Ryan looked up from behind the counter, a sly grin spreading across his face.

"Ah, Arlin! Right on time. I've got something to show you."

Arlin's curiosity was piqued. "What is it?"

Ryan chuckled. "All in good time, my young apprentice."

Just then, the door burst open, and Craig and Marliss tumbled in, laughing and arguing.

"Dude, I'm telling you, the best pizza topping is anchovies!" Craig exclaimed.

Marliss rolled her eyes. "You're insane, Craig. It's clearly mushrooms."

Arlin smiled, happy to see his friends. "Hey, guys! What brings you here?"

Craig spotted Ryan. "Oh, hey, Mr. Ryan! We're just grabbing a snack before our study group."

Marliss nodded. "Yeah, we're studying for our history exam."

Arlin's eyes met Ryan's, and they shared a knowing glance. Little did Craig and Marliss know, Arlin's "study group" was actually a magical training session.

Ryan smiled innocently. "Well, I won't keep you. Arlin, let's take a look at what I have for you."

As Ryan led Arlin to the back room, Craig called out, "Hey, Arlin! Don't forget to join us for pizza night tomorrow!"

Arlin grinned. "I wouldn't miss it."

The irony wasn't lost on Arlin. His friends thought he was just a bookworm, oblivious to his secret life as a wizard.

In the back room, Ryan revealed a small, ornate box. "This contains a magical tool that will aid you in your quest for the Orb of Light."

Arlin's eyes widened as he opened the box, revealing a beautiful crystal pendant.

Arlin's eyes sparkled as he held the crystal pendant, feeling an instant connection to the delicate, faceted stone. Ryan smiled, pleased with his apprentice's reaction.

"This is a Starlight Crystal," Ryan explained, his voice filled with reverence. "It's attuned to the celestial bodies and can amplify your magic. With this crystal, you'll be able to sense the Orb of Light's energy signature."

Arlin's mind whirled with excitement. "That means I can track it down!"

Ryan nodded. "Yes, but be warned, Arlin. The crystal's power comes with a price. You'll need to learn to control your emotions, or the crystal's energy can become unstable."

Arlin's determination hardened. "I'll learn to control it. I have to find that orb."

As Arlin left the shop, the crystal pendant safely tucked away in his pocket, he felt a sense of purpose. He was one step closer to saving his mother.

The sun was setting, casting a warm orange glow over the city. Arlin walked through the bustling streets, lost in thought. He stumbled upon a street performer, a musician playing a soulful melody on his guitar.

Arlin stopped to listen, entranced by the music. The notes seemed to resonate with the crystal's energy, and he felt a strange sense of harmony.

As the musician finished his song, Arlin applauded, feeling a sense of connection to the stranger.

"Thanks, man," the musician said, smiling. "You've got a good ear for music."

Arlin smiled back. "Thanks. I think the music just resonated with me."

The musician's eyes sparkled with curiosity. "Resonated, huh? You're a deep one, aren't you?"

Arlin chuckled. "I guess so."

As they parted ways, Arlin felt a sense of wonder. He realized that the crystal's power was not just about tracking down the Orb of Light, but also about connecting with the world around him.

Chapter 3

Arlin sat at his desk, the Starlight Crystal pendant glowing softly on his chest. He cracked open his laptop, the screen flickering to life as he booted up his trusty sidekick.

"Okay, Google," Arlin said, speaking into the microphone, "where can I find information on the Orb of Light?"

The search results poured in, and Arlin's eyes scanned the pages, taking in the various theories and legends surrounding the orb. He tweeted out a question on Twitter, hoping to crowdsource some leads.

"Hey, Twitterverse! Anyone know anything about the Orb of Light? DM me with any leads! #OrbofLight #Magic"

As he waited for responses, Arlin scrolled through Instagram, searching for any posts related to the orb. He stumbled upon a photo of an ancient text, the pages yellowed with age.

The caption read: "Just discovered this ancient text in the depths of the library! Could this be a clue to the Orb of Light's whereabouts? #OrbofLight #AncientTexts"

Arlin's eyes widened as he recognized the text. It was an ancient dialect, one that he had studied with Ryan.

He quickly DM'd the poster, asking for more information. As he waited for a response, Arlin fiddled with his Apple Watch, checking his notifications.

Suddenly, his phone buzzed. It was a text from an unknown number.

"Meet me at the old clock tower at midnight. Come alone."

Arlin's heart skipped a beat. Could this be the lead he was waiting for?

Arlin approached the old clock tower, the moon casting an eerie glow over the deserted streets. He checked his Apple Watch for what felt like the hundredth time, the display reading 11:59 PM.

As the clock struck midnight, a figure emerged from the shadows. Arlin's heart skipped a beat as the figure stepped into the light, revealing a young woman with piercing green eyes and jet-black hair.

"Who are you?" Arlin asked, trying to keep his voice steady.

"My name is Lyra," the woman replied, her voice husky and confident. "I've been searching for the Orb of Light for years. And I think I can help you find it."

Arlin's eyes narrowed. "What makes you think I'm looking for the Orb?"

Lyra smiled, a mischievous glint in her eye. "Let's just say I have my ways. I've been tracking your online activity, Arlin. You're quite the sleuth."

Arlin's face flushed with embarrassment. "You've been stalking me?"

Lyra chuckled. "I prefer the term 'researching.' But yes, I've been keeping tabs on you. And I must say, I'm impressed."

Arlin's mind whirled with questions. Who was this mysterious woman? And how did she know so much about him?

As they talked, Lyra revealed that she was an archaeologist, specializing in ancient civilizations. She had spent years studying the Tombs of Oriz, searching for any clues that might lead her to the Orb.

"The Tombs of Oriz are a labyrinthine complex," Lyra explained, her eyes sparkling with excitement. "They're filled with ancient artifacts, cryptic symbols, and hidden passageways. But I think I've finally cracked the code."

Arlin's ears perked up. "What do you mean?"

Lyra smiled, a sly smile spreading across her face. "I've discovered a hidden entrance to the tombs. And I think it might lead us straight to the Orb."

Arlin's heart skipped a beat. Could this be the break he was waiting for?

As they made their way to the Tombs of Oriz, Arlin couldn't help but feel a sense of excitement. He was finally one step closer to finding the Orb.

The Tombs of Oriz loomed before them, a sprawling complex of ancient stone structures. Lyra led the way, navigating the narrow passageways with ease.

As they walked, Arlin couldn't help but feel a sense of awe. The tombs were filled with ancient artifacts, cryptic symbols etched into the walls.

Lyra stopped suddenly, her eyes fixed on a small, intricately carved stone. "This is it," she whispered. "This is the entrance to the hidden passageway."

Arlin's heart skipped a beat. Could this be the moment he finally found the Orb?

As they made their way through the hidden passageway, Arlin couldn't help but feel a sense of trepidation. What lay ahead?

The passageway twisted and turned, leading them deeper into the heart of the tombs. Arlin's senses were on high alert, his magic at the ready.

Suddenly, Lyra stopped, her eyes fixed on a small, ornate box. "This is it," she whispered. "This is the box that contains the Orb."

Arlin's heart skipped a beat. Could this be the moment he finally found the Orb?

But as he reached for the box, Lyra's hand shot out, grabbing his wrist. "Wait," she whispered. "We're not alone."

Arlin's eyes narrowed. Who else was here?

As they stood there, frozen in anticipation, the sound of footsteps echoed through the passageway.

Arlin's magic surged to the forefront, his senses on high alert. Who was coming for them?

And what did they want?...

Arlin and Lyra exchanged a nervous glance. They were alone, the only sound the faint whisper of the wind through the passageway.

"Okay, here we go," Lyra whispered, her eyes fixed on the box.

Arlin nodded, his heart racing with anticipation. Together, they lifted the lid, revealing a glowing yellow cube nestled in a bed of velvet.

Arlin's eyes widened. "Uh, I think we were expecting an orb."

Lyra's face fell. "What is this thing?"

The cube pulsed with an otherworldly energy, emitting a low hum that vibrated through the air. Suddenly, ancient text erupted on the walls, scrolling by in a mad dash of hieroglyphics.

Arlin's eyes scanned the text, his mind racing to keep up. "Guys, I think we should—"

But it was too late. The cube burst into a blinding flash of light, and a voice boomed through the cavern, shaking the very foundations of the earth.

"I AM KORVUS, ANCIENT SORCERER OF THE YELLOW CUBE!"

Arlin stumbled backward, tripping over his own feet. Lyra grabbed his arm, pulling him upright.

"Uh, hi, Korvus?" Arlin ventured, trying to sound calm.

Korvus's voice was like thunder. "YOU DARE TO DISTURB MY REST? I WILL SHOW YOU THE TRUE MEANING OF POWER!"

The cube began to glow brighter, and Korvus's voice grew louder, more menacing. Arlin and Lyra stumbled backward, desperate to escape the sorcerer's wrath.

But it was too late. Korvus unleashed a blast of magical energy, sending Arlin and Lyra tumbling to the ground.

As they struggled to get back to their feet, Korvus's laughter echoed through the cavern, a cold, mirthless sound.

"You should not have disturbed my rest," Korvus sneered, his voice dripping with malice. "Now, you will never leave this place."

And with that, the cavern began to shake, the walls closing in on Arlin and Lyra. They were trapped.

Arlin groaned, rubbing his sore head. "Well, that didn't go as planned."

Lyra glared at him. "You think?"

As they sat there, trapped and helpless, Arlin couldn't help but wonder: what had they just gotten themselves into?

Arlin and Lyra huddled together, listening to the sound of Korvus's maniacal laughter echoing through the cavern.

"We have to get out of here," Lyra whispered urgently. "We can't let Korvus wreak havoc on the world."

Arlin nodded, his mind racing. "But how? The entrance is blocked."

Lyra's eyes scanned the cavern, searching for any possible exit. "We'll find a way. We have to."

Meanwhile, in the small town of Havenstead, Korvus was unleashing his full fury upon the unsuspecting residents.

The streets were filled with the sound of screams and shattering glass as Korvus summoned a maelstrom of magical energy, destroying everything in his path.

The townsfolk ran for their lives, desperate to escape the sorcerer's wrath. But Korvus was relentless, his power growing stronger by the minute.

A group of brave townsfolk, led by the local sheriff, attempted to stand against Korvus, but they were no match for his magical prowess.

As the town burned and the people fled, Korvus's laughter echoed through the streets, a cold, mirthless sound.

Arlin and Lyra, still trapped in the cavern, could feel the effects of Korvus's rampage. The ground shook beneath their feet, and the air was filled with the acrid smell of smoke.

"We have to stop him," Arlin said, his voice firm with determination.

Lyra nodded, her eyes flashing with resolve. "We will. We just need to find a way out of here."

As they searched for an exit, Arlin's mind turned to his friends, Craig and Marliss. Were they safe? Had they escaped the destruction?

Arlin's heart ached with worry, but he knew he couldn't give up. He had to find a way to stop Korvus and save the town.

But how?

Chapter 4

Arlin and Lyra emerged from the cavern, blinking in the bright sunlight. They had managed to escape, but not without triggering a magical alarm that would surely alert Korvus to their whereabouts.

"Come on," Arlin said, already moving towards Ryan's shop. "We need to get to Ryan's and figure out our next move."

Lyra followed closely behind, her eyes scanning the streets for any signs of danger.

When they arrived at Ryan's shop, the old wizard looked up from behind the counter, his eyes narrowing as he took in Lyra's presence.

"Who's this?" Ryan asked gruffly, his tone unmistakable.

Arlin hesitated, sensing Ryan's unease. "This is Lyra. We met in the cavern. She's been helping me search for the Orb."

Ryan's expression darkened. "I wasn't aware you were working with anyone, Arlin. Especially not someone I've never met."

Lyra stepped forward, her eyes flashing with defiance. "I assure you, Mr. Ryan, my intentions are pure. I'm only trying to help Arlin."

Ryan's gaze lingered on Lyra, his eyes searching for any signs of deception. "I'm not sure I believe you," he said finally. "Arlin, come with me."

Arlin followed Ryan to the back room, leaving Lyra alone in the shop.

"What's going on, Ryan?" Arlin asked, sensing his mentor's unease.

Ryan's expression was grim. "I think Lyra led you to Korvus on purpose. I think she's working with him."

Arlin's eyes widened in shock. "No, Ryan, that's not possible. Lyra's been helping me."

Ryan's gaze was unyielding. "I'm telling you, Arlin, something's not right. We need to be careful around her."

Arlin's mind reeled with uncertainty. Could Ryan be right? Was Lyra working with Korvus?

Arlin followed Ryan to the back room, where his mentor began rummaging through a dusty old trunk.

"What's going on, Ryan?" Arlin asked, curiosity getting the better of him.

Ryan pulled out a small, leather-bound book. "This is an ancient text on magical artifacts. I think it might hold some answers about the Starlight Orb."

Arlin's eyes widened as Ryan flipped through the pages. "What does it say?"

Ryan's eyes scanned the text. "It says that the Starlight Orb has the power to weaken a wizard's magic."

Arlin's eyes widened in shock. "That's why Korvus was so desperate to get it!"

Ryan nodded. "Yes, and it's also why we need to be careful around Lyra. If she's working with Korvus, she might be trying to get her hands on the orb."

Arlin's mind reeled with uncertainty. Could Lyra really be working with Korvus?

Ryan seemed to sense his unease. "Don't worry, Arlin. We'll figure this out together."

As they pored over the ancient text, Lyra walked into the back room, a cup of coffee in hand.

"Hey guys, I brought coffee," she said, setting the cup down on the table.

Ryan's eyes narrowed. "Thanks, Lyra. But I think we need to have a little chat."

Lyra's eyes sparkled with amusement. "Oh, this sounds serious."

Arlin rolled his eyes. "Ryan thinks you're working with Korvus."

Lyra's expression turned serious. "What? No, that's not true."

Ryan raised an eyebrow. "Then why did you lead Arlin to Korvus?"

Lyra sighed. "I didn't lead him to Korvus on purpose. I was trying to help him find the Orb."

Arlin's eyes met Lyra's, searching for any signs of deception. But all he saw was sincerity.

Ryan seemed to sense Arlin's uncertainty. "Let's not jump to conclusions. We need to do some research on Korvus."

Arlin nodded. "I'll start searching online."

Lyra pulled out her phone. "I'll check some ancient texts."

Ryan grumbled. "I'll go through my old books."

As they searched, the hours ticked by, the room growing quiet except for the occasional rustle of pages or tap of keys.

Finally, after what felt like an eternity, Lyra let out a triumphant cry.

"I found it!" she exclaimed, waving a dusty old scroll in the air.

Arlin's eyes widened. "What is it?"

Lyra unrolled the scroll, revealing a yellowed parchment covered in ancient text.

"It's a scroll from the ancient library of Alexandria," Lyra explained. "And it mentions Korvus."

Ryan's eyes lit up. "Let me see that."

As Ryan scanned the scroll, his expression grew grim.

"What is it?" Arlin asked, sensing his mentor's unease.

Ryan's eyes met Arlin's. "Korvus was once a powerful wizard, but he was corrupted by his own ambition. He made a pact with a dark entity, trading his soul for ultimate power."

Arlin's eyes widened in horror. "That's why he's so powerful."

Ryan nodded. "Yes, and that's why we need to stop him."

As they pored over the scroll, Arlin couldn't help but feel a sense of trepidation. They were in for the fight of their lives.

As they continued to study the scroll, Arlin's phone buzzed with a text from Craig.

"Hey, dude! What's up? We're still on for pizza night, right?"

Arlin smiled, feeling a pang of guilt for not telling his friends about his magical adventures.

"Yeah, I'll be there," Arlin replied, trying to sound casual.

Lyra raised an eyebrow. "Pizza night?"

Arlin nodded. "Yeah, my friends and I have a weekly pizza night. It's a tradition."

Ryan chuckled. "Well, I'm sure they have no idea what you're really up to."

Arlin grinned. "No, they don't. And I'd like to keep it that way."

As they continued to study the scroll, they discovered that Korvus's weakness was a magical artifact known as the "Eclipse Crystal."

"It's said to be able to absorb and nullify dark magic," Lyra explained.

Ryan nodded. "We need to find that crystal."

Arlin's eyes lit up. "I think I know where we can start looking."

With newfound determination, the trio set out on their quest to find the Eclipse Crystal and defeat Korvus.

As they left the shop, Arlin turned to Lyra and asked, "Hey, Lyra? Can I ask you something?"

Lyra smiled. "Sure, what is it?"

Arlin hesitated. "How did you know about the Starlight Orb? And how did you find that scroll?"

Lyra's expression turned serious. "I've been searching for the Orb for years. I've been studying ancient texts and scouring the globe for any clues."

Arlin's eyes narrowed. "And what about Korvus? What do you know about him?"

Lyra's eyes flashed with a hint of fear. "I know that he's powerful. And I know that he'll stop at nothing to get what he wants."

Arlin's grip on his backpack tightened. "We'll stop him. Together."

Lyra smiled, a hint of gratitude in her eyes. "Thanks, Arlin. I appreciate that."

As they walked, the sun began to set, casting a warm orange glow over the city.

Arlin felt a sense of hope. They might just have a chance to defeat Korvus after all.

But little did they know, Korvus was watching them from the shadows, his eyes burning with malevolent intent.

The battle was far from over.

Arlin, Lyra, and Ryan set out on their quest to find the Eclipse Crystal, determined to defeat Korvus and save the town.

Their first lead took them to an ancient temple on the outskirts of town, hidden deep within a dense forest.

As they navigated the treacherous terrain, Lyra suddenly stopped, her eyes fixed on a small inscription etched into the trunk of a nearby tree.

"What is it?" Arlin asked, following her gaze.

Lyra's eyes sparkled with excitement. "It's a riddle. It says:
'Where shadows dance, the crystal sleeps
Seek the reflection of the moon's soft beams'

Ryan's eyes lit up. "I think I know what it means."

Arlin raised an eyebrow. "What?"

Ryan smiled. "We need to find a place where the moon's light reflects off a surface, creating a shadowy pattern."

Lyra nodded. "And I think I know just the place."

They followed Lyra to a nearby lake, where the moon's light reflected off the calm water, creating a mesmerizing pattern of shadows and light.

As they searched the lake's edge, Arlin stumbled upon a small, hidden cave.

Inside, they found a pedestal, and on top of it, the Eclipse Crystal glowed with an otherworldly light.

But as they reached for the crystal, Korvus appeared, his eyes blazing with fury.

"You fools," Korvus spat. "You think you can defeat me? I have the power of the dark entity on my side."

Arlin stood tall, the Eclipse Crystal glowing brightly in his hand.

"We'll stop you, Korvus," Arlin said, his voice firm. "No matter what it takes."

And with that, the battle began.

NOW, LET'S EXPLORE Korvus's backstory:

Korvus was once a powerful wizard, renowned for his wisdom and magical prowess. However, as he delved deeper into the mysteries of magic, he became increasingly obsessed with gaining ultimate power.

One fateful night, Korvus stumbled upon an ancient tome hidden deep within the library's restricted section. The tome was bound in black leather, adorned with strange symbols that seemed to shift and writhe in the candlelight.

As Korvus opened the tome, he was met with a dark, malevolent presence that seemed to seep into his very soul.

The presence was that of the dark entity, an ancient being of immense power and malevolence.

Korvus, blinded by his ambition, made a pact with the dark entity, trading his soul for ultimate power.

And so, Korvus became a servant of the dark entity, using his newfound powers to spread darkness and chaos throughout the land.

But Korvus's thirst for power was never quenched. He continued to seek out new sources of magic, eventually leading him to the Starlight Orb.

And now, with the Eclipse Crystal in their possession, Arlin, Lyra, and Ryan were the only ones standing in Korvus's way.

ARLIN, LYRA, AND RYAN stood tall, ready to face off against Korvus. The air was electric with tension as the two sides clashed in a spectacular display of magic.

Korvus unleashed a barrage of dark energy blasts, but Arlin and his friends were quick to defend themselves. Lyra summoned a shield of swirling silver magic, while Ryan conjured a wave of fiery energy to counter Korvus's attacks.

Arlin, meanwhile, focused on harnessing the power of the Eclipse Crystal. He could feel its energy coursing through him, amplifying his magic and granting him newfound strength.

As the battle raged on, Korvus suddenly paused, his eyes locking onto Arlin's.

"You're just like me, Arlin," Korvus sneered. "Obsessed with magic, consumed by ambition. You'll never be satisfied with what you have. You'll always want more."

Arlin's eyes narrowed. "I'm nothing like you, Korvus. I'm not consumed by darkness and greed."

Korvus chuckled. "We'll see about that. You'll end up just like me, Arlin. Mark my words."

With that, Korvus resumed his attack, unleashing a devastating blast of dark energy that sent Arlin flying across the room.

As Arlin struggled to get back to his feet, Lyra and Ryan rallied to his side, their magic combining in a spectacular display of light and energy.

The battle raged on, the outcome hanging precariously in the balance. Would Arlin and his friends emerge victorious, or would Korvus's darkness consume them all?

AND NOW, LET'S EXPLORE the aftermath of the battle:

As the dust settled, Arlin, Lyra, and Ryan stood victorious, but battered. Korvus lay defeated at their feet, his dark magic dissipating into nothingness.

Arlin felt a mix of emotions: relief, exhaustion, and a hint of sadness. He had seen the depths of Korvus's darkness, and it had shaken him.

Lyra approached him, her eyes filled with concern. "Arlin, are you okay?"

Arlin nodded, forcing a smile. "Yeah, I'm fine. Just a little shaken."

Ryan clapped him on the back. "You did great, kid. We made a good team."

As they walked away from the battlefield, Arlin couldn't shake off Korvus's words. Would he end up like Korvus, consumed by ambition and greed?

He glanced at Lyra and Ryan, his friends and allies. He knew that with them by his side, he could face whatever challenges lay ahead.

But the seed of doubt had been planted, and Arlin couldn't help but wonder: what lay ahead for him, and would he emerge unscathed?

ARLIN, LYRA, AND RYAN returned to town as heroes, hailed by the locals for their bravery. They were showered with congratulations, pats on the back, and even a few awkward hugs.

As they celebrated their victory, Arlin couldn't shake off Korvus's words: "You'll end up just like me, Arlin. Mark my words."

He tried to push the thought aside, focusing instead on the festivities. But as the night wore on, his anxiety grew.

Finally, after what felt like an eternity, they made their way back to Ryan's shop. Arlin's stomach was growling, and he was looking forward to a well-deserved snack.

But as they arrived at the shop, Arlin's worst fears were confirmed. The Starlight Orb was missing.

Ryan's eyes widened in alarm. "It's gone! Korvus must have taken it."

Lyra's face fell. "But how? We defeated him."

Arlin's eyes narrowed. "I think Korvus faked his defeat. He used the Starlight Orb to temporarily weaken himself, making him untraceable."

Ryan's expression turned grim. "Which means he's on his way to find the Orb of Light."

The three of them exchanged a determined glance. The race was on.

"We need to move, now," Arlin said, already heading for the door.

Lyra and Ryan followed close behind, their faces set with determination.

As they disappeared into the night, the fate of the Orb of Light hung precariously in the balance. Would Arlin and his friends be able to find it before Korvus?

They made their way to the town's local café, where they gathered their gear and planned their next move.

Over a cup of coffee, Lyra pulled out a dusty old map, spreading it out on the table.

"Okay, so the Orb of Light is hidden in a temple deep within the Heartwood Forest," Lyra explained, tracing the route with her finger.

Arlin's eyes widened. "The Heartwood Forest? Isn't that, like, super dangerous?"

Ryan chuckled. "You have no idea."

Lyra shot him a withering look. "Hey, it's not that bad. We'll be fine."

Arlin raised an eyebrow. "You sure about that?"

Lyra nodded. "Positive."

As they set off towards the Heartwood Forest, Arlin couldn't help but wonder what lay ahead.

Would they make it to the temple before Korvus? And what dangers awaited them in the forest?

Only time would tell.

Chapter 5

Arlin, Lyra, and Ryan froze, their hearts pounding in unison. "What. Is. That?" Arlin whispered, his eyes fixed on the glowing orbs.

Lyra's voice was barely audible. "I don't know, but I think it's looking at us."

Ryan's eyes darted back and forth. "Yeah, and I think it's hungry."

The eyes drew closer, and Arlin could feel his breath catching in his throat.

Suddenly, a figure emerged from the shadows.

It was a towering creature with skin like bark and leaves for hair.

Arlin's eyes widened. "A tree person?"

Lyra elbowed him. "Shh, don't offend it."

The creature regarded them calmly. "I am Oakley, guardian of the forest."

Ryan stepped forward. "Uh, hi Oakley. We're just passing through."

Oakley's expression turned stern. "You should not have taken the shortcut. Now, you must pay the toll."

Arlin's eyes met Lyra's. "Toll?"

Lyra shrugged. "I think we're in trouble."

And with that, Oakley raised a branch, and our heroes prepared to face their fate...

ARLIN, LYRA, AND RYAN trudged through the Heartwood Forest, their senses on high alert for any signs of danger.

As they walked, Lyra suddenly stopped and consulted her map. "Guys, I think I found a shortcut."

Arlin's eyes lit up. "A shortcut? That sounds amazing."

Ryan raised an eyebrow. "What's the catch?"

Lyra hesitated. "Well, it's a bit more... treacherous."

Arlin grinned. "Treacherous? That's just a fancy word for 'fun.'"

Ryan shot him a withering look. "You're not exactly filling me with confidence, Arlin."

Lyra chuckled. "Come on, guys. It'll be fine. We can handle it."

And with that, they set off on the shortcut, which quickly proved to be a very bad idea.

The path narrowed, winding through a maze of twisted roots and overgrown underbrush. The air grew thick with the scent of decay and death.

Arlin stumbled, his foot catching on a hidden root. "Whoa, nice shortcut, Lyra."

Lyra shot him a sheepish grin. "Hey, I warned you."

Ryan muttered under his breath. "We're all going to die."

As they pressed on, the forest grew darker, the shadows deepening into menacing pools of blackness.

Suddenly, a twig snapped behind them.

Arlin spun around, his heart racing. "What was that?"

Lyra's eyes locked onto something in the distance. "I think we're about to find out."

And with that, a pair of glowing eyes appeared from the darkness, fixed intently on our heroes...

ARLIN, LYRA, AND RYAN froze, their hearts pounding in unison.

"What. Is. That?" Arlin whispered, his eyes fixed on the glowing orbs.

Lyra's voice was barely audible. "I don't know, but I think it's looking at us."

Ryan's eyes darted back and forth. "Yeah, and I think it's hungry."

The eyes drew closer, and Arlin could feel his breath catching in his throat.

Suddenly, a figure emerged from the shadows.

It was a towering creature with skin like bark and leaves for hair.

Arlin's eyes widened. "A tree person?"

Lyra elbowed him. "Shh, don't offend it."

The creature regarded them calmly. "I am Oakley, guardian of the forest."

Ryan stepped forward. "Uh, hi Oakley. We're just passing through."

Oakley's expression turned stern. "You should not have taken the shortcut. Now, you must pay the toll."

Arlin's eyes met Lyra's. "Toll?"

Lyra shrugged. "I think we're in trouble."

And with that, Oakley raised a branch, and our heroes prepared to face their fate...

Chapter 6

Arlin, Lyra, and Ryan studied the puzzle door, determined to unlock it.

Ryan's eyes sparkled. "I think I've got it! We just need to press the right sequence of stones."

Lyra nodded. "And I think I see the pattern. Let me try."

Arlin stepped back, watching anxiously. "Be careful, guys."

Lyra pressed the stones, and the door began to rumble.

Ryan grinned. "Yes! We did it!"

But instead of opening, the door started to glow with an eerie red light.

Arlin's eyes widened. "Uh, guys? I think we did it wrong."

The door exploded, sending rocks and debris flying everywhere.

Arlin, Lyra, and Ryan sprinted away, dodging falling rocks and leaping over chasms.

As they emerged from the dust cloud, gasping for breath, Arlin turned to his friends.

"Well, that was fun."

Lyra shot him a withering look. "You think that was fun?"

Ryan chuckled. "Hey, at least we made it out alive."

Arlin grinned. "Yeah, and we got a great story out of it."

But as they continued on their journey, they stumbled upon a sign that made their blood run cold:

"Welcome to the Lair of the Shadow Serpent."

Arlin's eyes met Lyra's. "You think that's a coincidence?"

Lyra's expression turned grim. "I don't believe in coincidences."

And with that, they steeled themselves for the dangers ahead...

Arlin, Lyra, and Ryan studied the puzzle door, determined to unlock it.

Ryan's eyes sparkled. "I think I've got it! We just need to press the right sequence of stones."

Lyra nodded. "And I think I see the pattern. Let me try."

Arlin stepped back, watching anxiously. "Be careful, guys."

Lyra pressed the stones, and the door began to rumble.

Ryan grinned. "Yes! We did it!"

But instead of opening, the door started to glow with an eerie red light.

Arlin's eyes widened. "Uh, guys? I think we did it wrong."

The door exploded, sending rocks and debris flying everywhere.

Arlin, Lyra, and Ryan sprinted away, dodging falling rocks and leaping over chasms.

As they emerged from the dust cloud, gasping for breath, Arlin turned to his friends.

"Well, that was fun."

Lyra shot him a withering look. "You think that was fun?"

Ryan chuckled. "Hey, at least we made it out alive."

Arlin grinned. "Yeah, and we got a great story out of it."

But as they continued on their journey, they stumbled upon a sign that made their blood run cold:

"Welcome to the Lair of the Shadow Serpent."

Arlin's eyes met Lyra's. "You think that's a coincidence?"

Lyra's expression turned grim. "I don't believe in coincidences."

And with that, they steeled themselves for the dangers ahead...

Chapter 7

Arlin, Lyra, and Ryan finally reached the inner sanctum of the temple, where the Orb of Light shone brightly.

Lyra's eyes widened. "It's beautiful."

Arlin smiled. "And it's ours."

But as they reached for the Orb, a voice echoed through the chamber.

"You'll never leave this place alive," Korvus sneered.

Arlin, Lyra, and Ryan spun around, their eyes locking onto Korvus.

He stood in the entrance, his eyes blazing with malevolent intent.

The final battle had begun.

Arlin, Lyra, and Ryan charged forward, their magic and swords at the ready.

Korvus retaliated with a wave of dark energy, but Arlin countered with a blast of light magic.

The battle raged on, the two sides exchanging blows and neither gaining the upper hand.

But as the fight wore on, Arlin began to tire.

Korvus sensed his weakness and pressed his advantage.

Arlin stumbled back, his vision blurring.

Lyra and Ryan rallied to his side, but even their combined strength couldn't hold back Korvus's onslaught.

Just when all seemed lost, Arlin remembered the words of the prophecy:

"The heart of light shall be the key."

With newfound determination, Arlin reached deep within himself and tapped into the heart of light.

A blast of energy exploded from his chest, striking Korvus with incredible force.

The dark sorcerer stumbled back, his eyes widening in shock.

Arlin took advantage of the opening, striking Korvus with a series of swift and precise blows.

Finally, with a cry of triumph, Arlin struck the final blow, defeating Korvus once and for all.

The temple began to shake, and the Orb of Light shone brighter, filling the chamber with an intense, blinding light.

And when the light faded, Arlin, Lyra, and Ryan stood victorious, the Orb of Light glowing brightly in Arlin's hand.

But as they turned to leave, Lyra's eyes met Arlin's, and he saw something there that made his heart skip a beat.

A spark of romance, ignited in the heat of battle.

Epilogue

Arlin, Lyra, and Ryan returned to Willowdale as heroes, hailed by the townspeople for their bravery.

As they celebrated their victory, Arlin's thoughts turned to his mother, still bedridden with the mysterious illness.

With the Orb of Light in hand, Arlin rushed to his mother's bedside, the orb's energy coursing through him.

He placed the orb on his mother's chest, and its light enveloped her, healing her wounds and restoring her vitality.

Arlin's mother smiled, her eyes shining with tears. "Arlin, my son, I'm so proud of you."

As the days passed, Arlin's mother regained her strength, and Arlin finally felt a sense of peace.

One evening, Lyra approached him, a mischievous glint in her eye. "Hey, Arlin, want to come to pizza night with me?"

Arlin's heart skipped a beat. Was this a date?

He grinned, trying to play it cool. "Sure, I'd love to."

As they sat down at the pizza parlor, surrounded by the warm glow of candles and the aroma of melting cheese, Arlin felt a sense of normalcy wash over him.

For the first time in months, he forgot about magic, and darkness, and ancient prophecies.

He just lived.

And as he glanced at Lyra, laughing and chatting with the other patrons, he knew that this was just the beginning of a new chapter in his life.

One filled with magic, adventure, and maybe, just maybe, a little romance.

As they finished their pizza and prepared to leave, Lyra turned to Arlin, her eyes sparkling.

"Want to walk me home?" she asked, her voice barely above a whisper.

Arlin's heart skipped another beat. This was definitely a date.

He grinned, feeling like the luckiest guy in the world. "I'd love to."

And as they strolled through the quiet streets of Willowdale, the stars shining above them, Arlin knew that he had finally found his place in the world.

A place where magic and adventure awaited, but also a place where he could find love, and friendship, and a sense of belonging.

THE END.

Next In The Arlin-verse

A promising wizard

EIRA

Eira Shadowglow, a brilliant and feisty archaeologist, stood at the edge of the dusty excavation site, her eyes scanning the horizon. The sun beat down on her, casting a golden glow over the sprawling ruins of the ancient city.

"DR. SHADOWGLOW, WE'VE found something!" her assistant, Jax, called out, waving a tattered map in the air.

EIRA'S HEART SKIPPED a beat as she strode over to Jax. "What is it?"

JAX HANDED HER THE map, yellowed with age and cracked with wear. Eira's eyes widened as she recognized the symbol of the ancient Eldarathians.

"THIS IS IT," SHE BREATHED. "This is the map to the lost city of Eldarath."

EIRA'S TEAM GATHERED around, their faces filled with excitement and curiosity. They had been searching for this map for years, and finally, they had found it.

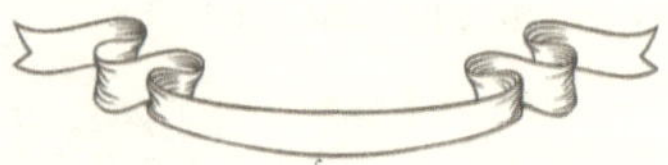

AS EIRA CAREFULLY UNFOLDED the map, she noticed a strange symbol etched into the corner. It looked eerily familiar, but she couldn't quite place it.

"JAX, DO YOU RECOGNIZE this symbol?" she asked, pointing to the marking.

JAX SHOOK HIS HEAD. "No, Doc. But it looks like some sort of code."

EIRA'S EYES SPARKLED with intrigue. "I think you're right. Let's get to work deciphering it."

AS THEY BEGAN TO STUDY the map and the symbol, Eira felt a shiver run down her spine. She had a feeling that this discovery was just the beginning of an epic adventure...

Eira poured over the map, her mind racing with possibilities. She had always been fascinated by the ancient Eldarathians, and now, she finally had a lead on their lost city.

AS SHE STUDIED THE symbol, she noticed a faint inscription etched into the edge of the map. "Jax, take a look at this," she said, handing him the map.

JAX EXAMINED THE INSCRIPTION, his brow furrowed. "It looks like an old dialect, but I think I can decipher it."

EIRA LEANED OVER HIS shoulder, watching as he worked. After a few minutes, Jax looked up, a triumphant grin on his face.

"I DID IT, DOC," HE said. "The inscription reads: 'Where shadows dance, seek the key.'"

EIRA'S EYES WIDENED. "That's it. That's the clue we need to unlock the code."

AS THEY CONTINUED TO study the map, Eira's mind wandered back to her childhood. She had grown up listening to stories about Arlin and his companions, who had saved the world from darkness.

HER GRANDMOTHER, A respected elder in their community, had been a close friend of Arlin's. She had passed down the stories, along with a few mysterious artifacts, to Eira.

EIRA'S CONNECTION TO Arlin's world ran deep, and she felt a sense of pride and responsibility to continue his legacy.

NOW, AS SHE GAZED AT the map, she knew that she was on the cusp of something big. Something that could change the course of history.

Also By Dylan Simphiwe Ncube

17 : THE AUTOBIOGRAPHY

Chapter 1

Welcome to my world.

Everyone else is busy having fun, me I'm having fun with the brand new Human synopsis and anatomy vol 2 textbook, it's the second thickest book in the school.

Well I presume you've already concluded that I'm a dork, well I'm not socially awkward. So let's rewind and see how I got here.

I'M NOT SURE IF I CAN still remember the timing in order but here's what I remember between the ages of 2-4.

Getting lost in a small city, my neighbor biting my chest, pooping in my porridge plate, being frightened by a frog at midnight and living with my uncles for a short period of time, breaking my arm.

Damn I was a lot .

NOW WHAT I REMEMBER almost clearly

It's my first day at school and my mom is walking me to class. The teacher introduces me to the other kids who are already whispering scazu. Damn I hate that name. It's elementary school so the day was never boring, I punched a guy in the face and he lost a tooth. I got hit by the teacher eight times for using foul language, at the age of six this seemed like a lot. I was an asthmatic so I kept getting told to wear my jacket at all times. Asthma is a respiratory problem not a some weather sickness. That's just some boring facts anyway. Well the next few days were fun until they told me we were having a race. Newsflash, I couldn't run because I was fat well I wasn't Rick Ross size but I was huge. I did run for a few meters and well my respiration wasn't so good so I had to slow down. Imagine my fastest speed was that of an athritic snail, how much slower could I go. The other kids opened up a gap larger than the one inbetween my ears.

I repeated the cycle for the next two to three years or maybe four.

It came to picking occupations everyone wanted to be a soldier (I'm still wondering what was going on the job is boring AF) so the teacher chose them for us. Guess who I became? President! Guess I always had aura since I was a kid, they gave me the most powerful role in the country.

I did great at roleplay, well I had superb memory.

I didn't know the correct units of time but I always remembered all the details. God! I wonder where all that went. Back to the script I was still illiterate at the time so we'd to memorize our lines which was like cutting margarine with a hot knife. I also had love for musical instruments, the guitar mostly, I still want one. Then it came to drawing, we were told to choose from a series of objects in the room. Pick one and draw, I tried to imitate a Jesus poster well it came out right, if he'd been attacked by zombies, put in a car crusher and then presented. I picked up the art later in my early high school years. I did a couple cartoons before I lost it again.

My most important asset was violence. I was used to living with my uncles who watched too much Jackie Chan movies. Damn I almost became the karate kid. Anyway I kicked a lot of butt sometimes self defense and most of the times I just enjoyed beating others guess that's why everyone wanted to beat me once I lost power. I punched at least seventy percent of my classmates . I wasn't a bully I just enjoyed superiority and it helped my case if everyone thought I was Russia in human form. I also enjoyed watching wrestling and I had the opportunity to practice new moves on my peers, that is if I had any. I decided to practice a superkick on a third grader named Brian. I landed my foot on his face he was taller and three years older than me and that just made me the GOAT.

Until first grade where I lost one fight. Just one fight was enough to take down the whole British empire. I fell off like Drake after the beef with Kendrick. Which was a steep slope in my combat stats. After that I lost most of the respect I had obtained from the poor humans. I did one heroic act that saved the entire school from going home late.

ENGLISH IS A PROBLEM to most Zimbabweans. For Three centuries it has been a big one. Fluency would have made you get respected like you won a Nobel prize. The problem was simple, the headmaster was asking a question which I didn't understand. Everyone else understood it but could not answer in ENGLISH. I wasn't even supposed to be at school by that time but my brother had just been transferred to my school so I hanged out with him a lot. Even went to some sporting activities with him. Back to the problem, everyone was given an opportunity and failed. Then the headmaster decided to bring the big guns, THREATS . Well one threat, he said no one would leave the school premises until he's answered correctly. That just led to mumbling amongst students. Well I decided it was to late so I confidently stood up and yelled "Kill me like a tree!". Pause. And then distinct chatter. They were forced to applaud, and there I stood like superman after saving the metropolis. Hands on my waist, chest out,chin up and legs spread evenly to my sides. Classic superhero look, I just didn't have a red cape and boots plus I have knock knees. Who am I kidding I looked like Rod Wave tryna jump off an airplane, or maybe a Black version of Lance Barber (The guy who played Sheldon's father in Young Sheldon. But the confidence was real. Everyone went home and I became the talk of the week.

They need school magazines at primary schools. Who's going to keep an archive of the best school experiences if we don't have those. Imagine a magazine article with the title KILL ME LIKE A TREE SAYS A SIX YEAR OLD BOY. Okay ,that sounds lame now that I'm saying it out loud .

Coming soon

Don't miss out!

Visit the website below and you can sign up to receive emails whenever Dylan Simphiwe Ncube publishes a new book. There's no charge and no obligation.

https://books2read.com/r/B-A-QRHLC-UTOLF

BOOKS 2 READ

Connecting independent readers to independent writers.

Did you love *Arlin*? Then you should read *17* by Dylan Simphiwe Ncube!

Read more at https://leansavagemerch.teemill.com/.

Also by Dylan Simphiwe Ncube

Treats For Young Readers Series
The Magic Paintbrush
Arlin

Watch for more at https://leansavagemerch.teemill.com/.

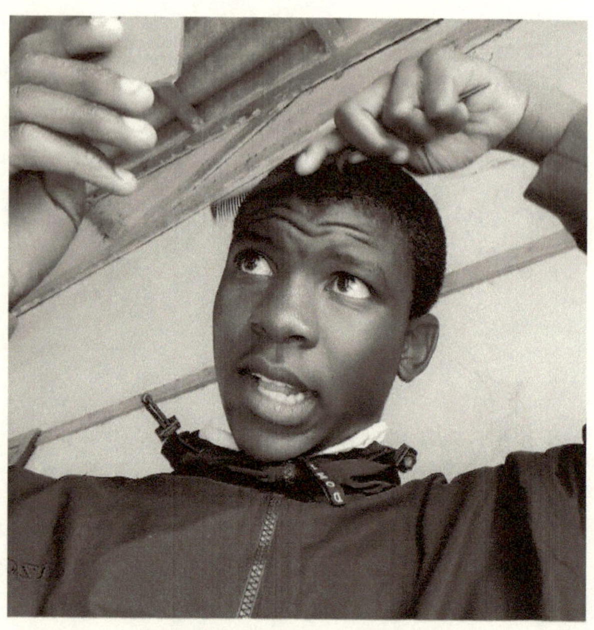

About the Author

Dylan Simphiwe Ncube better known as Lean Savage is a Zimbabwean Rapper, Singer Songwriter Record Producer and Writer.

He was born on the 11th of October 2006.

He has switched hobbies ever since.

As of now he is a student doing his A level.

More work should be expected including an Autobiography

Read more at https://leansavagemerch.teemill.com/.

About the Publisher

Part and under authority from Leanshake Records LLC, created by and managed by Dylan Simphiwe Ncube and crew

www.ingramcontent.com/pod-product-compliance
Lightning Source LLC
Chambersburg PA
CBHW021135130726

47988CB00003B/1312